MEET THE
NEIGHBORS

ISBN: 0-439-87509-9

Over the Hedge TM & © 2006 DreamWorks Animation L.L.C.

Published by Scholastic Inc.
SCHOLASTIC and associated logos are trademarks and/or registered trademarks of Scholastic Inc.

12 11 10 9 8 7 6 5 4 3 2 1   6 7 8 9 10/0

Designed by Paul W. Banks
Printed in the U.S.A.
First printing, May 2006

MEET THE NEIGHBORS

ILLUSTRATIONS BY PETE EMSLIE
AND KOELSCH STUDIOS

SCHOLASTIC INC.

NEW YORK   TORONTO   LONDON   AUCKLAND   SYDNEY
MEXICO CITY   NEW DELHI   HONG KONG   BUENOS AIRES

*R*J the raccoon was hungry. He wanted food and he wanted it now. RJ knew where to find some food—even if it belonged to a mean, sleeping bear. RJ crept into the bear's cave and quietly loaded a pile of food into a wagon.

It would have been a clean getaway but **RJ** couldn't resist sampling some chips from his haul. The can opened with a pop and a hiss.

Vincent the bear opened a yellow eye. RJ panicked. The wagon full of food rolled down the hill and was hit by a truck.

"I'm waking up again in one week," Vincent growled. "And all my stuff had better be right back where it was."

The next morning, one woodland family woke up to the first day of spring.

"Only 274 days left until winter!" Verne the turtle warned as everyone ran off to look for food.

Hammy the squirrel didn't find any food. He found something very tall and very green, stretching as far as he could see. He showed it to the other animals. They were scared . . . very scared.

Finally, Verne worked up his courage, and pushed through the thing to the other side.

erne entered a strange new world. A hundred houses stood where the woods had been. As Verne explored, he discovered frog-shaped water sprinklers, sharp barbecue tools, and a writhing garden hose that flung him over a fence, where he plopped into a toy **SUV**. He careened down a driveway and straight into the path of a life-size **SUV**.

"**AAAAAH!**" Verne howled as he shot under the huge car.

BAM! He hit a mailbox, landing in the street next to a hockey puck.

FWAP! A roller-skating human slap-shot Verne back into the forest.

Verne told the animals that humans and houses had taken away half the forest. The animal family worried how they would gather enough food for the winter.

RJ had been watching the animals from a nearby tree. Their troubles gave him an idea about how to repay Vincent. He hopped down and told the animals that the big green wall was called a hedge, and that on the other side they would find lots of food that they could store for winter. Like chips!

The animals ate nacho chips. They loved the cheesy goodness.

RJ took the animals through the hedge that night. "Welcome to suburbia," he cried. Everywhere the animals looked, humans were eating. And the stuff they didn't eat? "They put it in gleaming, silver cans, just for us!" RJ said triumphantly. "Dig in!"

uddenly, a huge cat came out of a house, took one look at the animals, and let out a bloodcurdling, "MEEEEOOOWWWW!"

Then, a woman, Gladys, burst out, waving a broom.

"Get out of here!" she screamed, swinging wildly.

The animals ran back through the hedge, breathless and terrified.

"We want nothing to do with ANYTHING that's over that hedge," Verne insisted.

But RJ had only one week to get enough food to pay back Vincent. He had a new plan, and he needed Hammy's help.

The very next day, RJ lured Hammy over the hedge.

"I WANT MY COOKIES!" Hammy screeched.

He jumped up and down in front of two Trail Guide Gals who had been peacefully delivering cookies until this crazy animal appeared. They watched in horror as Hammy ran around in circles like a maniac, trying to scare them.

Finally, the girls bashed Hammy over the head with their manual.

Hammy was in big trouble until Verne came to his rescue. But RJ looked like the hero when he returned to the forest with a big wagonful of cookies.

The heists continued as the animals took food, toys, and games from the humans. Everyone was having fun. Everyone except Verne. He didn't trust RJ. Then, one day, Verne heard the sound of screeching tires. He raced to the road. Ozzie the possum was lying "dead" on the pavement.

It was just a trick so the animals could steal a blue cooler that RJ secretly needed for Vincent. Gladys was fed up. She called an exterminator—Dwayne LaFontaine—who immediately set up an enormous system of animal traps.

Verne knew that as long as the animals and RJ took food from the humans, they would never be safe. RJ knew it too and tried not to care.

Verne decided the only way to protect his animal family was to return the food to the people. RJ was determined to stop him—he had only a few days left to bring the wagon full of food to Vincent! The two began pushing and pulling at the wagon.

"Play! Play! Play!" said Nugent the dog, who had been chained in the backyard. He chased them and the wagon all over the neighborhood. Finally, the wagon snagged on a gas canister that exploded and sent the wagon, Verne, and RJ rocketing skyward. It crash-landed, destroying everything.

he rest of the animals blamed Verne for the lost food and sided with **RJ**.

"You're taking advantage of them," Verne yelled at **RJ**, "because they're too stupid and naïve to know any better!"

As soon as he'd said it, he was sorry. Verne didn't mean to hurt his animal family.

The animals glared at Verne. Then they turned and walked slowly away.

*V*erne finally admitted it. He was jealous of RJ and how quickly RJ had become the family's leader. He and RJ had a long talk. They agreed to work together to get the food back so the animals would have plenty to eat in the winter.

The animals planned their biggest heist yet. They had to get inside Gladys's house. But they needed the cat's collar, because it opened the automatic door like a key.

"Stella, you will get that cat to give you his collar by using . . . "

"My stink," said Stella.

"No, your feminine charms!" RJ corrected.

It was extreme makeover time for Stella.

iger found Stella so charming that getting his collar was easy. She distracted him while the animals snuck through the pet door and into Gladys's house.

Inside, they moved fast. The wagon soon filled up and they were ready to scram. Then RJ saw a can of Vincent's favorite potato chips on a high shelf.

He knew he couldn't leave without it.

"We have enough food!" Verne insisted.

"Hey, listen, I've got to deliver these chips to a homicidal bear!" RJ snapped.

Finally Verne understood what RJ was really up to. But there was no time to fight.

ladys had seen the animals and she had called Dwayne! Captured in a net and thrown into the back of Dwayne's truck, the terrified animals awaited their fate.

All except **RJ**. He had gotten away with the wagonload of food. Now everyone knew he'd wanted it all for himself from the very start.

J quickly delivered the food to Vincent. "I stopped to watch the show," growled the bear.

RJ looked down the hill and saw that his friends were in trouble.

He knew what he had to do.

RJ grabbed the wagon and rode it down the hill, crash-landing into the truck. Dwayne was knocked out. Verne ended up in the driver's seat, but he had no idea what to do. Luckily, the porcupine kids took over the steering wheel. It was just like one of their new video games.

incent chased after **RJ** and landed on the truck. "AAAAH!" the animals screamed as the truck swerved wildly, flew into the air, and crashed into Gladys's house like a meteorite.

Dwayne and Gladys chased the animals into the hedge. Vincent grabbed at them from the forest side of the hedge. They were trapped.

It was time for action. It was Hammy Time. Hammy was a speeding blur as he raced across the yard, pushed the animal trap's **ON** button, and bolted past the motion sensors, back to the hedge.

Seconds later, Vincent lunged at RJ, crashed through the hedge, and landed in Gladys's backyard. Before anyone could react, the trap exploded, leaving Vincent, Gladys, and Dwayne caught in a smoking cage.

KA BOOM

$\mathcal{B}$ack in the forest, the animals were celebrating. RJ watched them.

"Hey RJ," Verne said. "If you had told us that you owed food to a bear, we would've just given it to you! That's what families do."

"This whole family thing is very confusing," RJ said.

"Wanna be part of it?" Verne asked with a smile.

RJ definitely did. It was time for a group hug.